The
Griffin
and
Oliver Pie

To Finley
Before you get too old

ORCHARD BOOKS
338 Euston Road, London NW1 3BH
Orchard Books Australia
Hachette Children's Books
Level 17/207 Kent Street, Sydney, NSW 2000

First published in Great Britain in 2006

A CIP catalogue record for this book
is available from the British Library.

ISBN 1 84362 356 0

1 3 5 7 9 10 8 6 4 2

Printed in Great Britain

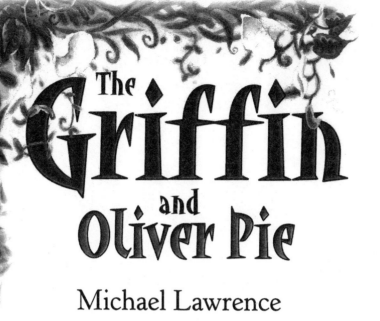

The Griffin

and Oliver Pie

Michael Lawrence

Illustrated by

Adam Stower

ORCHARD BOOKS

Contents

The Guardian
of Hidden Treasures

Oliver Pie sat on the back step in the sunshine and sighed for the thirteenth time in five minutes. They were going to Uncle Martin's and Auntie Linda's for the day, and his father was still upstairs ironing his favourite awful shirt, and his mother was putting one of her faces on, and Oliver Pie had been ready for *ages*.

Oliver Pie looked very smart today. His hair was just so, and he was wearing his best clothes and the belt with the big silver buckle his gran had given him on her last visit. Oliver Pie hated dressing up and looking all neat, but he was very fond of his new belt, and would have worn it all the time if he was allowed, except in bed and the bath.

Sitting on the back step in the sunshine waiting for his parents, Oliver Pie tilted his toes this way; then he tilted them that way; then he leaned back to see how the sun shone on his silver belt buckle.

But then he remembered he was bored and sighed for the fourteenth time and looked up the garden, hoping to see something interesting.

It wasn't a very large garden and it wasn't a very tidy garden, and there was a high old crumbly old wall round it, and right down the bottom there was a little wooden door. Oliver Pie hadn't known about the door till yesterday when his mother had cleared some of the ivy away from the high old crumbly old wall; and suddenly there it was, just begging to be opened. His mother *had* opened it, and she'd looked through, but then she'd said, 'Yes, well I think we'll pretend it doesn't belong to us,' and shut it again before Oliver Pie could run up and see for himself.

Oliver Pie, sitting on the back step in his best going-to-see-people clothes, looked up the garden at the little wooden door in the high old crumbly old wall.

'Hmm,' he said, and got up slowly and wandered down the garden pretending to swat flies.

When he reached the little wooden door Oliver Pie turned and looked at the house to make sure no one was watching while he fiddled behind his back with the big round handle. 'Just a peek,' he said, tugging at the handle. 'That's all, just a little peek.'

The door creaked and groaned and opened a crack, and Oliver Pie looked through. And what a disappointment! There was nothing there. Nothing at all but long grass and weeds, then more long grass and more weeds.

Or so he thought.

'Hello?' said a very deep, very old voice.

Oliver Pie jumped. He looked harder. But as hard as he looked there was still nothing to see but long grass and weeds, then more long grass and more weeds.

'Who's that?'

'Oh, I'm nobody,' the deep old voice replied. 'Can't be, or I wouldn't have been left alone out here all these years, talking to myself.'

The voice seemed to come from a small hill some way into the wild garden that his mother wanted to forget about. Oliver Pie swished towards it.

'Still can't see you,' he said when he got there.

'Well you wouldn't,' snapped the deep old voice, 'with all this stuff on top of me.'

Oliver Pie tugged at some of the grass and weeds that covered the small hill. Underneath he found something ancient and bumpy, and surprisingly cold to the touch for such a warm day.

A large grey wing.

'You'll find another one of those on the other side,' the voice said. 'If you can be bothered to look, that is.'

Oliver Pie went round the other side and

uncovered the second wing. It fluttered a little, even though it was made of stone.

'If you'd do the same for my head,' the stone creature said, 'you would make me very happy. I can't tell you how I long to see the sun again.'

Oliver Pie cleared the grass and weeds away from a grey stone head with a great curved beak. A large eye blinked at him.

'A boy, if I'm not mistaken,' said the owner of the eye, the beak and the wings. 'Can't remember the last time I saw a boy. Or any other creature come to that, other than snails, slugs and spiders. What are you called, boy?'

'Oliver Pie,' said Oliver Pie. 'What about you?'

'What do you mean, what about me?'

'I mean what's your name?'

'I don't have a name,' the stone creature said. 'Only humans have names. Silly habit if you ask me.'

'Well what are you then? An eagle?'

The stone creature looked offended. 'Did you come out here to annoy me, Oliver Pie, because if so I'd rather you went back where you came from and forgot we ever met.'

'Sorry,' said Oliver Pie.

'And I am most definitely not an eagle. An eagle is a mere *bird*, while I...'

A feathery stone chest lifted a little from the weeds. 'I am a *griffin*. I would have thought that was obvious.'

'What's a griffin?'

'Don't be ridiculous, everyone knows what a griffin is.'

'I don't,' said Oliver Pie.

The griffin clucked his beak, but raised his head proudly. 'A griffin is a Guardian of Hidden Treasure.'

Oliver Pie's mouth fell open. 'You mean there's *treasure* under here?'

'Er, well, no, not exactly,' the griffin answered, somewhat less proudly. 'You see I've been moved.'

'Moved?'

'Yes. New people took over the house when my maker died and they can't have liked me much because they put me out here, beyond the wall, where I couldn't be seen. I've been here ever since, unwanted, neglected, forgotten. It's a lonely life.'

But then the griffin heaved a contented sigh and gazed about him.

'Oh, but this sunshine. *Wonderful* after all this time.'

'Would you like me to clear some more weeds away?' Oliver Pie asked.

The griffin's stone eyelids fluttered in surprise.

'Why, how kind. Yes I would. I'd really be most grateful.'

Older than Grandpa

Oliver Pie got to work, and very soon he saw that the griffin, in spite of his wings and beak and the talons of his forelegs, was indeed much more than an eagle. There were just a few feathers on his back, for instance, and his hindquarters and legs were like a lion's. He even had a lionish tail.

The griffin stretched his stone wings with pleasure.

'I wouldn't do that if I were you,' said Oliver Pie. 'Bits of you fall off when you move.'

'Bits would fall off you too if you were as old as me,' the griffin replied.

'How old is that?'

'Very old. Very, *very* old.'

'As old as my grandpa?'

'Oh, even older I should think. So many suns have set and moons risen since the master mason made me.'

'What's a master mason?' Oliver Pie asked.

'A man who carves wondrous things out of stone,' the griffin informed him. 'You don't know much, do you, Oliver Pie?'

'No, I don't suppose I do. Sorry.'

'Well, you're only human,' he said magnanimously. 'And I can forgive anyone who wears such a magnificent belt.'

Oliver Pie looked at his new belt. 'My gran gave it to me. I like the buckle, don't you?'

'Oh I especially like the buckle. It must be nice to have a gran. I never did. Stone creatures don't, usually. I was very fond of my maker, though. He used to come and sit beside me in the evenings and talk to me. I was his finest creation, he often said so.' The griffin tilted his head to catch the best of the sunlight. 'Am I still handsome? Am I still a delight to the eye, a wonder to behold?'

'Well,' said Oliver Pie.

'It's all right, you can tell me, I'm not vain. You know, in my day–'

The griffin's voice was drowned out by a terrible roar from high above which cast a long white trail across the sky.

'In *my* day,' he repeated irritably, 'there were no flying monsters making a dreadful racket and interrupting civilised conversations between a griffin and his admirer. Not counting dragons, of course.'

Oliver Pie's eyes popped. 'Were there

really dragons once upon a time?
My dad says there was never any such thing.'

'Dads don't know everything,' the griffin
said. 'They think they do, but they don't.
They never did, it's a myth.'

'Oliver Pie!
What on earth
are you doing
out here?'

Oliver Pie
jumped. His
mother stood
all hunched
over in the
little wooden
doorway in
the high old
crumbly
old wall.

'Mum!
Look what
I've found!'

His mother swished through the long grass and weeds and stared at the griffin, who was now perfectly still, eyes looking at nothing.

'Well! All the time we've lived here – almost a year now – and we had no idea there was anything like *this* out here!'

'You might have had if you'd taken the trouble to look,' said a sour, whispery old voice that only Oliver Pie could hear.

'He's a griffin,' said Oliver Pie.

His mother glanced at him in surprise. 'How do you know that?'

'He told me. And he's even older than Grandpa!'

'Golly.' His mother walked round the griffin, touching him here and there with her fingertips. 'Wait till your dad sees this.'

'He says he's a...a Garden of Hidden Treasure. Or he would be if he hadn't been moved.'

'Fancy that,' Mum said, not really listening. 'Well, we'll have to decide what to do about him some other time or we'll be late for...' She frowned. 'Oliver Pie, you're wearing your best shoes!'

'You told me to.'

'Yes, but I didn't know you'd be wandering about out here, did I? Come on, to the kitchen, they'll need a rub up.'

His mother swished away through the long grass and weeds and ducked through the little wooden door in the high old crumbly old wall.

'Got to go now,' Oliver Pie said to the griffin.

The griffin blinked at him. His eyes were even larger all of a sudden.

'Of course you have. Everyone leaves me sooner or later. Well, who am I? Just an old griffin without any treasure to guard. But it's all right, I'm used to it. You run along and enjoy yourself.

Don't spare me another thought.'

'I'll come back tomorrow after school,' Oliver Pie said. 'Promise.'

'Suit yourself,' the griffin said, and looked away. 'It's all the same to me.'

A New Home

At school next day, during lunch break, Oliver Pie suddenly felt as sad as sad can be. He'd eaten half his packed lunch and was kicking a ball about with Thomas, Joe and Adam, and his sadness put him right off his game.

'You're useless today, Oliver Pie!' said Thomas.

'Can't play for toffee!' said Joe.

'My hamster could play better than you!' said Adam.

He went on feeling sad all afternoon, and everyone noticed.

'Cheer up, Oliver Pie,' his teacher said. 'You'll have us all in tears in a minute.'

'Yes, Mrs Walker.'

'Let's see a smile then.'

'Yes, Mrs Walker.'

Oliver Pie smiled, but it wasn't a real smile, and Mrs Walker changed the subject to keep everyone from bursting into tears. It was while Mrs Walker was busy changing the subject that the thought came to Oliver Pie that his sadness might be to do with the griffin. And once he'd thought that, he couldn't wait to get home.

When his father met him after school, Oliver Pie ran up to him eagerly and said, 'Dad, Dad, is the griffin all right?'

'Hello Dad,' said Dad. 'Good to see you, Dad, and what sort of day have you had, Dad? Oh, mustn't complain, Oliver Pie, thanks for asking.'

Oliver Pie gripped his father's hand and hauled him towards their house.

'Is the griffin all *right*?!' he repeated.

'He's fine,' said Dad, who'd only met the griffin just before breakfast that morning. 'So fine, in fact, that you might get that new bike you've been after.'

Oliver Pie frowned suspiciously.

'What's the griffin got to do with a new bike?'

'The money I got for him. New bike for you, new nightie for Mum, new mouse mat for me.'

'What do you mean, the money you got for him?'

'I've sold him,' said Dad, unlocking the front door and looking very pleased with himself.

Oliver Pie tumbled inside and sat down hard on the chair in the hall.

'You've sold the *griffin*?'

His father followed him in and closed the door.

'I was down at the garden centre this morning and I bumped into Mr Moss, the owner, and told him about the griffin. He asked if he could come and take a look at it, and when he came round he made me an offer. An hour later some men were here loading it onto a truck. Did you know that in olden times stone griffins were placed over treasure, to guard it?'

Oliver Pie leapt to his feet in a fury.

'*What did you have to go and sell him for?!*'

'Well he wasn't much use to us, was he?' his father said, taken aback. 'We haven't got any treasure to guard. But now that he's sold we have enough for a new bike, a nightie and a mouse mat. I thought you'd be pleased.'

'Pleased?' yelled Oliver Pie. 'He was my new friend! You've sold my *friend*!'

'Oh,' said Dad. 'Sorry. Didn't realise you were so attached.'

Oliver Pie scowled up at him with his hands in fists.

'I want to see him. I want to see him *now*!'

'Well, I can take you to see him,' Dad said, 'but I can't get him back.'

'Why not?'

'I've already bought the mouse mat.'

*

They found the griffin easily enough. There were a lot of flowers and pot plants in this corner of the garden centre, and a gushing ornamental fountain which people tossed coins into for luck. The griffin stood in pride of place with a number of other statues, much newer statues, and he was the only one that wasn't for sale, which made him very special.

Oliver Pie ran to the griffin. 'Oh, Griffin,' he said, 'I'm sorry, I'm sorry, I didn't know my dad would *sell* you!'

He stroked a crumbly old wing, but the griffin wouldn't look at him or say a word. When Oliver Pie listened very closely he heard a small griffinish sigh, but that was all.

'Looks good here, doesn't he?' his father said, catching him up. 'Not as pretty as some of the new statues, but not at all...oh!'

'Oh what?' said Oliver Pie.

'Feel sort of…gloomy all of a sudden.'

'It's the griffin. He's sad about being here instead of in our garden.'

Just then two small boys ran up to look at the griffin. They were laughing as they approached, but as they drew near they fell silent. For a second or two they just stood there, staring at him. Then they burst into tears.

Their mother rushed to them. 'What's the matter with you two?'

They couldn't tell her because they didn't know. All they could say was that they felt miserable. And then, as she comforted them, tears sprang into their mother's eyes too. 'What *has* come over us?' she said. 'I think we'd better go to the café and find something to cheer ourselves up, don't you?'

As they moved away, the boys' smiles came back, and then they were laughing again, and running on ahead to the café. Their mother glanced about in embarrassment, hoping she hadn't been seen. Then she smiled again too.

'Weird,' said Dad, watching them go.

'It's the griffin,' said Oliver Pie again. He leaned close to the griffin's ear. 'Aren't you talking to me?' he whispered.

This time the griffin did reply. He said: 'No.'

And that's all Oliver Pie could get out
of him.

A Favourite Spot

When his father met him from school the next day, Oliver Pie refused to speak to him. Even when Dad gave him a bar of chocolate he'd bought at the corner shop (which he was only supposed to do on Fridays) he bit into it in silence with his nose in the air.

The first thing he did when they got home was go out to the little wooden door in the high old crumbly old wall and look through. Perhaps the griffin had come back somehow. He hadn't, of course.

Oliver Pie closed the door and went to his favourite spot in the garden by the house. The favourite spot was a ring of sunflowers. Because they were sunflowers the sun shone more brightly on them than on anything else. It was very private and peaceful in the ring of sunflowers. The cat liked to curl up in there and snooze, and sometimes Oliver Pie hid there, or just sat inside the ring being quiet and warm and golden.

But when he went into the sunflower ring today it wasn't to hide or to be quiet. He just wanted to feel a bit happier. The sun shone as brightly as ever on the heads of the tall yellow flowers, but his happiness did not come back. How could it come back when the griffin was gone and he was going to have an operation tomorrow?

I don't think I've told you about Oliver Pie's operation. Well, Oliver Pie had been having a lot of sore throats lately, and a bit of trouble breathing, and the doctor had said that his annoyeds had to come out. They were actually called adenoids, but Oliver Pie called them annoyeds because that was how he felt about having to go to hospital with them. If the griffin had still been there, Oliver Pie would have told him all about this, and perhaps it wouldn't have been so bad then. But the griffin wasn't there.

When his mother came home from

work, Oliver Pie said: 'Mum, can we go to the garden centre? I've got to tell the griffin something.'

But Mum shook her head. 'Sorry, can't be done. Things to get ready for tomorrow, and then there's the tea to make, and we can't go after tea because it's your dad's computer course at the college and he'll have the car.'

Oliver Pie sulked till teatime. Then he sulked during tea. Then he watched a bit of telly and sulked till the adverts came on. Then he began to worry about the operation and got upset, so his mother wrapped him in her big old cardigan with the holes in the elbows, and they watched one of his videos together until he fell asleep, and that was it until morning when he started worrying all over again.

There were four beds in the hospital room, but only two were occupied, one by a small boy who slept most of the time, the other by Oliver Pie. Oliver Pie's mother, who was a nurse on another ward, had gone to find him a book or comic to keep him occupied. While he waited for her to come back, Oliver Pie lay all alone thinking how hungry he was. He hadn't had any breakfast. Hadn't been allowed any because Mum said you weren't supposed to eat before an operation.'It's not fair,' Oliver Pie said, screwing up his eyes.

'Life isn't,' said a gloomy voice. 'Or I'd still be guarding my Hidden Treasure instead of at *that* place being pointed at and crawled over by small humans.'

Oliver Pie unscrewed his eyes.

'Griffin!'

'Ssssh,' said the griffin. 'Someone might hear you.'

Someone had. A nurse put her head round the door.

'You all right, precious?'

'I think she means you,' said the griffin to Oliver Pie.

'Yes, thanks,' said Oliver Pie to the nurse.

'Well just shout if you need anything.'

And the nurse went away again.

'She didn't say anything about you,' Oliver Pie said to the griffin.

'She couldn't see me. No one can, here, except you.'

'Why can I see you and no one else can?'

'Because that's the way I want it,' the griffin said.

'Oh,' said Oliver Pie. 'Why are you here anyway?'

'I had a feeling you'd be glad of my illustrious company.'

'You weren't talking to me the day before yesterday.'

'That was the day before yesterday,' said the griffin.

'Won't they miss you at the garden centre?'

'Oh, I'm still there too. It's possible for a griffin to be in two places at once, you know – if he has a mind to.'

'Clever,' said Oliver Pie.

'I am,' said the griffin.

'Griffin...'

'Yes?'

'Were you frightened of things when you were little?'

'I was never little. I was always the size I am now. I was new once, though, and when I was new I didn't know what things were about, so I suppose you could say I was a bit *nervous* sometimes.'

'I wish I'd known you when you were new,' Oliver Pie said wistfully.

'Do you?' the griffin said, with some surprise.

'Yes I do,' said Oliver Pie.

'Well if you *really* wish it,' the griffin said, 'I can show you.'

'Show me what?'

'Myself, when new. I can take you back to when I was just made.'

'You can do *that?*' said Oliver Pie, impressed.

'Well I've never done it before,' said the griffin, 'but I don't see why I couldn't now that you're here. It takes two for a wish to work properly, you see. Would you like to go?'

'Well I *would,*' said Oliver Pie, 'but my mum's only gone for a comic or something and she might miss me.'

The griffin shook his head. 'You'll be back in the wink of an eye, before anyone knows you've gone.'

'All right then,' said Oliver Pie.

'Place your hand on my wing,' the griffin instructed him. 'Then we must both close our eyes and wish to see me when I was new and even more wonderful to behold.'

So Oliver Pie put his hand on one of the griffin's wings, and they both closed their eyes and wished to see the griffin when he was new and even more wonderful to behold. For a few moments he felt as if he was floating in nothing, but then...

'There,' the griffin said. 'I knew I could do it. There's life in the old stone yet.'

Oliver Pie opened his eyes. Gone was the hospital room, gone were the four beds and the little boy sleeping in one of them. The griffin and Oliver Pie (in his pyjamas and bare feet) stood in a small yard outside a large house. There were no flowers or trees in the yard, only round grey cobbles, with a stable to one side.

'Do you know where we are?' the griffin said.

'No,' said Oliver Pie.

'Look harder.'

Oliver Pie looked about him once more. And frowned. Then he walked (with some difficulty seeing as his feet were bare) across the hard cobbles to a spot where the sun shone with particular brightness.

'This is like the place where the sunflowers grow, and the cat likes to snooze, and where I hide sometimes when Mum calls me for bed.'

'Whatever it becomes some day,' the griffin said, 'it will first be the place where my master buries his treasure. The place where I will stand guard – until I'm moved out of sight anyway.'

The Wink of an Eye

Oliver Pie looked again at the house with the cobbled yard, and parts of it began to seem familiar. It was much newer than the house he'd lived in for a year, differently shaped here and there, and some of the windows were in the wrong place. There were also two tall chimneys he'd not seen before, but—

'It's where I live with my mum and dad and our cat and some spiders!'

'Where you will live,' the griffin said. 'One day, when I'm older than your grandpa.'

Chip-chip. Chip-chip.

'What's that?' said Oliver Pie.

'Why don't we go and see?'

It didn't seem strange to Oliver Pie that the griffin was able to move; for here, though still made of stone, he was much more like a living breathing creature. He followed the griffin through the broad open door of the house, into a shadowy workshop full of stone animals and birds, and great pots and gateposts, and slabs with words cut into them. By a small window a broad-shouldered man chipped away at an enormous piece of stone. There was a slight hump on the man's back and his thick beard was grey with dust.

'It's him,' the griffin said softly. 'My maker. I haven't seen him for an age. Several ages actually.'

'Is it all right for us to be here?' Oliver Pie whispered.

'He can't see or hear us. We're here by magic, invisible to his eyes, silent to his ears.'

Chip-chip. Chip-chip.

Suddenly the man set his tools aside and sat back, stretched his arms and shoulders, his work completed. Now they could see the thing he'd been working on.

'Griffin,' said Oliver Pie. 'It's…you.'

Together they inspected the brand new wings, the great proud beak, the clawed front feet, the lionish hindquarters and tail.

'What a handsome chap I was,' the griffin said.

'You don't look very alive though,' said Oliver Pie.

'It wasn't until I was put outside, in my place over the treasure, that life entered me,' the griffin informed him. 'It goes with the job. There's no point in being a Guardian of Hidden Treasure if you're a cold dead thing, is there?'

'What's he doing now?' asked Oliver Pie

The mason had risen and crossed the room, and now he knelt before a little metal door in the wall. He unlocked the door and took out a small iron casket, which he carried to his workbench by the window.

'It's the treasure,' the griffin said. '*My* treasure.'

They looked over the mason's shoulder as he threw back the lid of the little casket and began removing the contents piece by piece, breathing on each item in turn and buffing it up on his sleeve. It wasn't a great treasure, nor a very sparkly treasure; there weren't masses of bright coins and rubies and amethysts and sapphires and diamonds and gleaming silver goblets; but there were necklaces and rings, and half a dozen large brooches, and a number of small pieces of beaten copper that glinted in the light.

'Most of these belonged to his wife,' the griffin said. 'Some he made himself, specially for her. When she died he locked them all away because it saddened him to see them and know that she could not.'

'And this is the actual treasure he buried under you?'

'It is. He wanted to be sure it would be kept safe. And it would have been, to this day, if people who came after him hadn't moved me.'

'Perhaps it's still there,' said Oliver Pie.

'I doubt it,' the griffin said. 'I was moved such a long time ago, and humans do tend to poke around and find things.' He sighed to think of his lost treasure. 'Well,' he said then, 'time to go.'

'So soon?'

'Time can be made to pause, but she's an impatient mistress. She won't wait long, even for griffins. The wink of an eye is almost up.'

The mason was still looking sadly through the treasure he'd decided to bury in the yard under his splendid new griffin. The old griffin leaned towards him and gently touched his forehead with his beak. The mason didn't appear to feel anything, but a small smile twitched his

lips when the griffin whispered tenderly:
'Goodbye, Father.'

Then the griffin turned to Oliver Pie.

'Place your hand on my wing now, close
your eyes, and we'll wish to be back at
the hospital.'

'I don't want to go back to the hospital,'
said Oliver Pie.

'You must,' said the griffin.'

So Oliver Pie put his hand on one of the griffin's ancient wings and closed his eyes and reluctantly wished to be back at the hospital.

When he opened his eyes he was in bed again and Mum was just coming in the door with something for him to read.

But the griffin had gone.

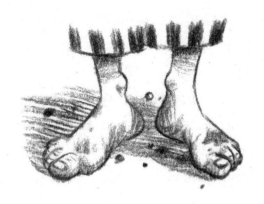

Tonsils Too

About an hour before the operation a nurse put some thick cream on the back of Oliver Pie's hand, with a see-through plaster on top. Oliver Pie pressed the plaster and it went all squishy. Shortly after that, his mother asked him if he wanted to go to the toilet. Oliver Pie said yes he did, and got out of bed. Mum stared at the soles of his feet.

'Oliver Pie, where have you *been*?'

'The mason's house.' he told her, turning his feet round to look at them over his shoulders. 'I saw the griffin when he was new.'

'Well it's a pity you didn't wear your slippers. You can't go for your operation like that. We'll have to wash them.'

So they went to the toilet and while they were there Mum washed Oliver Pie's feet (but not in the toilet). When they came back they found two people waiting for them. One was the nurse who'd put the squishy plaster on, and the other was a porter. The porter had brought a very high bed with wheels to take him to the operation room.

The nurse asked Oliver Pie if he was ready and Oliver Pie said 'No,' and the nurse laughed, and she and Mum lifted him – 'A-one, a-two, and up-we-go!' – onto the very high bed. Then Mum and the nurse and the porter wheeled him out of the room and along some corridors until they came to a lift.

They all crowded into the lift and went up to a small room, where the nurse removed the squishy plaster from the back of Oliver Pie's hand and Oliver Pie said, 'Is that it? Can I go home now?'

'Not *quite* yet,' said a tall man in a green jacket and green trousers who'd just come in. 'Chat to Mum for a while.'

The tall man in green took the hand that the squishy plaster had been on, and Mum took the hand that hadn't had a plaster, and she and Oliver Pie chatted for a while until he began to feel sleepy. But then, just before he drifted off, his mother's voice turned into someone else's.

'Don't worry, Oliver Pie, I'm here. Everything's all right now, don't worry, don't worry...'

Oliver Pie sighed, glad that the griffin had come to be with him for the operation, and went to sleep.

*

'Hello,' said a voice. Not the griffin's. Oliver Pie's eyes opened all by themselves and saw Mum sitting on a chair beside his bed – his ordinary hospital bed, the one without wheels. She was still holding the hand that hadn't had a plaster.

'Have my annoyeds gone?' Oliver Pie asked in a croaky little voice.

'Yes, all gone.'

'But my throat's even *sorer* now!'

'That's because you've had your tonsils out as well.'

'My tonsils? Why?'

'Because the annoyeds were what made it hard for you to breathe and the tonsils were what gave you all those sore throats.'

'But I've still *got* a sore throat,' said Oliver Pie.

'You will have for a day or two,' his mother said. 'But then you'll be as good as new, you see if you're not.'

'No I won't. I won't have my tonsils any more. You shouldn't have taken my tonsils out without asking.'

'We couldn't ask. You were asleep.'

'You should have waited till I woke up,' he said. 'They were my tonsils, and…and I miss them.'

The Big Day

Next morning, when it was time to go home, Oliver Pie's father came for him in the car. Mum had to stay behind at the hospital, so she waved them off from the main entrance and blew kisses. Oliver Pie scowled. He'd told her *so many times* not to blow kisses when other people were about.

The hospital had given him a badge and a certificate to prove that he'd had an operation and been brave. 'You can wear the badge to school,' Dad said on the way home. 'And I'll have the certificate framed so everyone will know what a hero you were.'

'I'm still not talking to you properly,' croaked Oliver Pie.

'Because your throat hurts or because I sold the griffin?'

Oliver Pie folded his arms and stuck his bottom lip out and looked straight ahead. 'Griffin,' he grunted.

The first thing Oliver Pie did when they got home was go upstairs to look at his room and bounce on his comfortable bed. The second thing he did was go down again, then out to the garden, to the place where the ring of sunflowers grew and the sun shone with particular brightness. But he didn't step inside the circle today. He just stood there looking at the tall flowers with their big bright heads. After a while he went to the shed, lugged out an enormous spade, and called his dad.

'What's the spade for?' Dad said when he came out.

'You've got to dig down under the sunflowers.'

'Why?'

'Because there might still be treasure there. There was when the griffin was here.'

'The griffin wasn't here. He was on the other side of the wall in the wild garden.'

'Before he was put *there*,' Oliver Pie said impatiently, 'he was *here*, guarding the mason's treasure.'

'You know this for a fact, do you?' his dad said.

'Yes,' said Oliver Pie. 'He told me.'

'Well in that case we'd better take a look.'

Now as you may know, dads don't usually dig up their gardens just because

their sons tell them to, but this dad still felt
a bit guilty about selling the griffin, and he
wanted to be friends again. So he lifted
some of the sunflowers and laid them
carefully aside, intending to put them
back once he'd dug down
and not found
treasure.

He dug down quite a way, stopping frequently to mop his brow because he wasn't used to hard work. Twice he said, 'There's nothing here,' and each time Oliver Pie told him to dig a bit deeper. So he dug on, and on – and suddenly the spade struck something. Something that clanged.

'That'll be it,' said Oliver Pie.

'Probably just a lump of rock,' said Dad.

But he got down on his hands and knees and cleared the earth away. It wasn't a lump of rock. It was a small iron casket.

'Told you,' said Oliver Pie.

His father lifted the box out with amazement.

'But how did you..? I mean how could you possibly...?'

The mason's casket didn't open easily. It had been down there since the griffin was new and was thick with rust. Dad went for a screwdriver and gently forced the lid back. They looked inside.

There it was, the mason's treasure, just as Oliver Pie had last seen it, only duller and older. He looked through the necklaces and rings and brooches, and the small pieces of beaten copper that no longer glinted in the light, then he said: 'Better put it back now.'

'Put it back?' his father said. 'You're kidding me.'

'It's not ours. It's the mason's. I just wanted to see if it was still there, and now I can tell the griffin and perhaps he'll be pleased.'

'But this is a real find,' Dad said. 'It may not look much, probably won't make anyone rich, but the museum might be glad of it.'

'The museum?' said Oliver Pie with interest. The museum was one of his favourite places to visit.

'You've seen the sort of stuff they have on display. They love things like this. Be a real treasure trove to them, this will.'

'Would it be safe at the museum?'

'Safe as houses. Everything's kept under lock and key, and guarded by a man in a blue uniform with a cap. And you can go and see it whenever you like.'

Oliver Pie thought this over for a while. Then he said: 'I'll have to see what the griffin thinks.'

'Oh yes, we must see what the griffin thinks,' said Dad. 'After lunch, eh?'

'But this is important,' said Oliver Pie.

'I've got ice cream for afters. Bought it specially, to soothe your throat. Strawberry, vanilla and chocolate, with wafers to scoop it up.'

'I don't like vanilla,' said Oliver Pie.

'Swap your vanilla for my strawberry,' Dad said.

Oliver Pie thought about this. Then he said: 'All right. But straight after lunch – OK?'

'You're the boss,' said Dad.

What the Griffin Thought

Straight after his chocolate and double strawberry ice cream, Oliver Pie put on his new belt with the big silver buckle and went with his dad to the garden centre. The griffin was still in the same place near the fountain, surrounded by other statues and flowers. But how dull everything looked today! The flowers were pale and limp, the gush of the fountain was reduced to a mere trickle, and those of the statues that had faces looked very down in the mouth.

While his father wandered about looking at boring things like pots and compost and fencing, Oliver Pie put his arm round the griffin's neck and said how glad he was to see him and that he was

wearing his new belt with the big silver buckle specially.

The griffin stared grimly ahead of him. 'Hm! Aren't you going to say hello, how are you, Oliver Pie?' said Oliver Pie with his new husky voice.

'I know how you are,' the griffin muttered out of the side of his beak.

'How can you know?'

'I'm a griffin. I'm wise.'

Oliver Pie stroked his beak.

'I know you are. You're the wisest griffin in the whole world, and you're my favourite too.'

The eye nearest to him wobbled a bit, and almost looked at him. 'You don't know any others.'

'No, but if I did you'd still be my favourite. Why are you in a bad mood again? You were all right yesterday, at the hospital and the mason's.'

'It's this place,' mumbled the griffin. 'It gets me down. People keep pointing at me. Pointing and prodding. And children clamber up on me. It's not *dignified*.'

A middle-aged couple stopped to look at the new statues. 'Grumpy looking lot, aren't they?' the man said. 'Wouldn't want any of them in my gar...' He shivered suddenly. 'Chilly here.'

His wife shivered too. 'Funny, it's warm enough everywhere else. And I feel quite...sad.'

'So do those flowers by the look of them,' her husband said. 'Look as if they won't last the day.'

They moved off. Oliver Pie noticed that once they were a short distance away they brightened up.

'You're making people unhappy,' he said to the griffin.

'That's because *I'm* unhappy.'

'Well I've got something cheerful to tell you. Good news.'

The griffin's head turned a little towards him.

'Good news? For me? I don't believe you. I never get good news.'

'I've found the mason's treasure,' said Oliver Pie. 'It was still there, where he put it.'

The stone wings jumped. A hanging basket went flying. The griffin was suddenly very interested indeed.

'Still there? After all this time?'

'Yes! And my dad thinks we should give it to the museum.'

The griffin's head reared back. 'I beg your pardon? Do my ears deceive me? Did you say give my treasure *away*? To a...*museum*?'

'He says it'll be safe as houses in the museum,' Oliver Pie said. 'It'll be *guarded*.'

'Not by me it won't,' scowled the griffin.

'No, but there's a man there in a blue uniform with a cap, which means he's good at guarding things. And it wasn't being guarded before, was it, so it must be better off there.' He leaned closer, hopefully. 'Don't you think? Griffin?'

The griffin turned aloofly away. 'Why ask me? You seem to have made your mind up. Well why shouldn't you? I'm nobody. Just an old stone statue. I don't have to be asked if I mind what happens to *my* treasure.'

As he said this several things happened. The fountain sputtered and the mere trickle of water became an even merer trickle. More flowers wilted – so badly that a number of them lost all their petals at once – and cracks appeared in three of the statues, and two arms and a leg snapped off.

'*Please* cheer up!' Oliver Pie cried in alarm. 'You'll get us into trouble.'

'Don't want to cheer up,' said the griffin sulkily.

'Griffin, listen. If the treasure's in the museum we can go and look at it whenever we want. We couldn't do that if it was buried again, could we? We could go together, you and me, by your magic – couldn't we?'

The griffin sniffed haughtily and some of his stone feathers lifted. 'I wash my claws of the matter. You must do as you see fit.'

Which Oliver Pie took for permission to give the treasure to the museum. When it was time to go he promised to come again tomorrow and tell him what had happened about it.

'I wouldn't bother,' the griffin said mournfully. 'Why worry about a lump of old stone that serves no useful purpose? No, you run along and find something more interesting to talk to. A wall, for instance.'

'Oh Griffin,' said Oliver Pie.

'I'll be all right,' the griffin went on. 'I'm used to being alone with no one to talk to. I'll just sit here, day after day, year after year, while my bits drop off one after the other. Then one day someone will come and sweep up the last of me, and that'll be that. No more griffin.' He sighed heavily. 'I don't suppose I'll be missed.'

Three old ladies passing by burst into tears. A head toppled off a statue. The griffin closed his eyes.

Moved Again

Next day, Oliver Pie's throat was still sore and a bit croaky. Dad brought him some breakfast in bed, on a tray, which Oliver Pie liked so much that he asked if he could have it every day. Dad said, 'Don't push your luck, kid.'

But even better than breakfast in bed on a tray was Mum coming home just before lunch and saying she'd got the afternoon off and was taking Oliver Pie out for a treat.

77

Oliver Pie got dressed in his second best clothes and he and his mum went out and had lunch at a café. Then they looked round some shops and Mum bought him a new football because the old one wasn't as big as it used to be.

When they got back home Dad came rattling down the stairs from his little office at the top of the house where he messed about with his computer.

'Guess what,' he said.

'Did you tell the museum about the treasure?' Oliver Pie asked.

'Yes, someone's coming to look at it. Should be here any minute. But what I was going to say was—'

The doorbell rang before he could finish. It was the man from the museum. He was a small man with a large moustache and when he saw the treasure in the mason's rusty old casket the moustache went all bristly and his eyes lit up.

'Oh my,' he said. 'Well now. Wow. Yes indeedy.' He looked at Oliver Pie. 'Your father tells me you found it in the garden.'

'Yes, the griffin used to guard it before they moved him.'

'The griffin?'

'My friend,' said Oliver Pie.

'Oh,' said the man, but he was too fascinated by the mason's treasure to think about griffins. He told Oliver Pie and his parents that the museum would be honoured to have the treasure, and that it would probably be given a glass case all of its own.

'I think we ought to put a special notice in with it,' he added. 'Something like: "This treasure was discovered by Oliver Pie." How's that?'

'There should be something about the griffin too,' said Oliver Pie.

'I'll see what I can do,' said the man from the museum.

He made a list of everything in the casket and handed the list to Oliver Pie to look after, and then he took the mason's treasure away with him, casket and all.

'You'll be famous,' said his mum.

'So will the griffin,' said Oliver Pie. 'Can we go to the garden centre and tell him?'

'Er, no,' said Dad. 'That's what I was going to tell you. He's not there any more.'

Oliver Pie gulped. 'Not there?'

'Mr Moss phoned just after you went out to tell me there'd been complaints from customers that they got depressed when they went near the griffin. Not only that, but the plants all round him were dying, statues were falling apart, and the fountain had stopped working.'

'So he got rid of him?' said Oliver Pie. 'Just like that?'

'Just like that,' said Dad.

A lump jumped up into Oliver Pie's throat and his heart tumbled down into his trainers. The griffin wasn't even at the garden centre now! He would never see him again – ever!

But then something happened. Something odd. He felt himself perking up. He couldn't understand it. The griffin was gone forever and he was...happy.

How awful! How *unkind*!

'Why don't you go into the garden?' his father said.

'Don't want to go into the garden,' said Oliver Pie, trying to frown. 'I'm upset.'

'All the more reason to go,' said Dad. 'The garden is the best place to be when you're upset. Trust me, I know about these things.'

So Oliver Pie headed for the garden. He went dragging his feet to keep them from skipping, which is what they seemed to want to do. But when he stepped outside, when he stood in the garden, he knew immediately why he felt happy and stopped feeling bad about it. He wasn't even angry that Dad hadn't put back the sunflowers he'd dug up to get at the treasure. For there, in the remaining half circle of sunflowers...

'Griffin!'

Oliver Pie ran to him and flung his arms round his knobbly old neck.

'Griffin, you're back, and in your proper place, where the treasure was!'

'So I am,' the griffin said. 'If the treasure had been here too everything would have been perfect, but...ah well, one should count the few blessings one has, I suppose.'

'You're not going all gloomy again, are you?' said Oliver Pie. 'If you go all gloomy the flowers might droop like at the garden centre, and I don't like droopy flowers.'

'The flowers won't droop,' said the griffin. 'Not now that I'm back in my rightful place. Look!'

Oliver Pie looked. The sun fell across the garden like a golden umbrella, and all the flowers seemed bigger and brighter and bolder than ever. Even the sunflowers that had been dug up and left on the ground didn't look too unhappy.

New Treasure

Just before bed that night Oliver Pie went out to the garden in his pyjamas and slippers. It was getting dark, but the moon cast a silver gleam upon the griffin's beak and wings. He looked very grand in the moonlight. The half circle of sunflowers standing tall behind him looked like the high back of a great throne.

Oliver Pie had a carrier bag with him, and a big spoon from the kitchen.

He bent down and started digging between
the griffin's front feet with the spoon.

'What are you doing?' the griffin asked.

'Digging a hole,' said Oliver Pie.

'Why? What for?'

Oliver Pie opened the carrier bag and
took out a carved wooden box. He'd bought
the box at the Oxfam shop some time ago
with his birthday money. He opened
the box and the griffin
looked inside.

It contained Oliver Pie's special treasures; things people had given him that he wanted to keep, or which he'd got from Christmas crackers or won at the fair.

'Nice things,' the griffin said.

'They're for you,' said Oliver Pie.

'Me?' said the griffin.

'Oops,' said Oliver Pie. 'Almost forgot the most important thing.'

From his dressing gown pocket he took the big silver buckle from the belt his gran had given him on her last visit, and put it in the Oxfam box.

'Oh, Oliver Pie,' said the griffin.

Oliver Pie closed the box and placed it in the hole he'd dug between the griffin's feet. The griffin dipped his head and watched him cover the box and pat the earth down on top with the big spoon from the kitchen.

'There,' whispered Oliver Pie. 'Now you have hidden treasure to guard again.'

The Guardian of Hidden Treasure lifted his head. His great wings spread and rippled like the waters of a stone lake. He stood very tall in the semi-circle of sunflowers and the moonlight, and his beak curved ever so slightly, ever so proudly.

'I shall guard it well,' said the griffin to Oliver Pie.

Turn the page to
find some more books
by Michael Lawrence
that you might enjoy…

Something's after Jiggy McCue!
Something big and angry and invisible.
Something which hisses and flaps and stabs
his bum and generally tries to make
his life a misery. Where did it come from?

Jiggy calls together the Three Musketeers
– One for all and all for lunch! –
and they set out to send the poltergoose
back where it belongs.

Shortlisted for the Blue Peter Book Award

The underpants from hell – that's what
Jiggy calls them, and not just because they look
so gross. No, these pants are evil.
And they're in control. Of him. Of his life!
Can Jiggy get to the bottom of his
problem before it's too late?

"...the funniest book I've ever read."
Teen Titles

"Hilarious!"
The Independent

Winner of the Stockton Children's
Book of the Year Award

Feel like your life has gone down the pan?
Well here's your chance to swap it
for a better one!

When those tempting words appear on the
computer screen, Jiggy McCue just can't resist.
He hits "F for Flush" and...Oh dear.
He really shouldn't have done that.
Because the life he gets in place of his
own is a very embarrassing one – for a boy.

"Fast, furious and full of good humour."
National Literacy Association

"Altogether good fun." ***School Librarian***

"Hilarity and confusion." ***Teen Titles***

£4.99

1 84121 756 5

Michael Lawrence

Jiggy McCue wants some good
luck for a change.
But instead of luck he gets a genie.
A teenage genie who turns against him.
Then the maggoty dreams start.
Dreams which, with his luck and this
genie, might just come true.

"Will have you squirming with horror and delight!"
Ottakars 8-12 Book of the Month

"Funny, wacky and lively."
Cool-reads

MORE STORIES FROM
ORCHARD BOOKS

Jiggy McCue stories by Michael Lawrence

☐ The Poltergoose   1 86039 836 7   £4.99

☐ The Killer Underpants   1 84121 713 1   £4.99

☐ The Toilet of Doom   1 84121 752 2   £4.99

☐ Maggot Pie   1 84121 756 5   £4.99

☐ The Snottle   1 84362 344 7   £4.99

☐ Nudie Dudie   1 84362 647 0   £4.99

☐ Neville the Devil   1 84362 879 1   £5.99

☐ Ryan's Brain   1 84616 227 0   £5.99

☐ Billy Bonkers by Giles Andreae   1 84616 151 7   £4.99

☐ Snakes' Elbows by Deirdre Madden   1 84362 640 3   £4.99

Do Not Read . . . by Pat Moon

☐ Do Not Read This Book   1 84121 435 3   £4.99

☐ Do Not Read Any Further   1 84121 456 6   £4.99

☐ *Do Not Read – Or Else*   1 84616 082 0   £4.99

Jamie B stories by Ceri Worman

☐ *The Secret Life of Jamie B – Superspy*   1 84362 389 7   £4.99

☐ *The Secret Life of Jamie B – Rapstar*   1 84362 390 0   £4.99

☐ *The Secret Life of Jamie B – Hero.com*   1 84362 946 1   £4.99

Red Apple books are available from all good bookshops, or can be ordered direct
from the publisher: Orchard Books, PO Box 29, Douglas, IM99 1BQ.
Credit card orders please telephone 01624 836000 or fax 01624 837033 or email:
bookshop@enterprise.net for details.

To order please quote title, author and ISBN and your full name and address.
Cheques and postal orders should be made payable to 'Bookpost plc'. Postage and
packing is FREE within the UK (overseas customers should add £1.00 per book).
Prices and availability are subject to change.